THIS BOOK BELONGS TO:

_____

_____

To Lucy and Mary.

© Text: Gilberto Mariscal, 2017
© Illustrations: María Jesús Jiménez, 2017
© This edition: Curvilínea S.L., 2017

Printed by CreateSpace

www.chuwydesign.com
info@chuwy.es

If
Santa
didn't have his sleigh

GILBERTO MARISCAL

ILLUSTRATED BY CHUWY

WWW.CHUWYDESIGN.COM

Lucy and Mary loved Christmas.

Firstly, because they had no school.
They were on holidays!

Secondly, because the street lights
brightened up the sky at night.

And thirdly... because on Christmas Eve Santa Claus comes with his Christmas presents!

However, the day before Christmas Lucy seemed very worried:

"Are you sure Santa is coming tonight?" she asked her mother.
"Of course, Lucy. He will come on his sleigh from the North Pole, and he will bring many gifts to all the children of the world and... to you!"

"But... what if Santa didn't have his sleigh?"
"Well! That is a good question... Lucky I know the answer! I will tell you the story!" her mother replied smiling.
"Yes, yes!" Lucy and Mary celebrated.

"If Santa didn't have his sleigh, he would bring gifts to all the children of the world on... **his magical Bicycle!**" their mother revealed to Lucy and Mary.

"Bike!" Mary repeated.

"But... what if the wheels of the magical Bicycle puncture?" Lucy asked.

"Don't worry" her mother replied, "If Santa didn't have his sleigh, nor his magical Bicycle, he would take the gifts to all the children of the world in... **his noisy Car!**"

"Brooooooom!" Mary roared.

But Lucy was not very convinced:
"And what if the noisy Car breaks?" she asked.

"If Santa didn't have his sleigh, nor his magical Bicycle, nor his noisy Car, he would bring the gifts to all the children of the world in... **the Christmas Train!**" her mother replied.

"A train! Woo... woo!" Mary sang.

However, Lucy still doubted: "What if Santa runs out of coal in the Christmas Train and it stops? Then he could not get to our house!"

"Do not worry Lucy, he will come." Her mother reassured her: "Because if Santa didn't have his sleigh, nor his magical Bicycle, nor his noisy Car, nor his Christmas Train, he would bring gifts to all the boys and girls of the world in... his **multi-coloured Balloon!**"

"Multi-coloured? Wow!" Mary exclaimed happily.

To Lucy, on the contrary, the story seemed increasingly strange:

"And what if the multi-coloured Balloon deflates?" she asked seriously.

"If Santa didn't have his sleigh, nor his magical Bicycle, nor his noisy Car, nor his Christmas Train, nor his multi-coloured Balloon, he would bring gifts to all the boys and girls of the world in... **his super-fast Plane!**"

Lucy hesitated, suspicious:

"If the Plane crashes... how will Santa bring us gifts? On a boat?"

"Yes! How did you know Lucy?" her mother said.

"If Santa didn't have his sleigh, nor his magical Bicycle, nor his noisy Car, nor his Christmas Train, nor his multi-coloured Balloon, nor his super-fast Plane, he would bring gifts to all the children of the world in... **his pirate Ship!**"

"But... what if the boat sinks?" Lucy insisted.

"If Santa didn't have his sleigh, nor his magical Bicycle, nor his noisy Car, nor his Christmas Train, nor his multi-coloured Balloon, nor his super-fast Plane, nor his pirate Ship, he would bring gifts to all the boys and girls of the world on... **a giant Whale!**"

"On a Whale? I don't believe that! How is Santa going to bring gifts to our home if whales can not walk?"
Lucy asked.

"It is very simple, Lucy" her mother explained, "The magical Doves of Christmas will pick Santa up from the shore and help him carry his presents to all the children of the world."

"Do magical Doves exist?" Lucy asked.
"Of course!" her mother assured her.

But Lucy was reluctant to give up:

"And what if the magical Doves of Christmas get sick and can not take Santa?"

"If Santa didn't have his sleigh, nor his magical Bicycle, nor his noisy Car, nor his Christmas Train, nor his multi-coloured Balloon, nor his super-fast Plane, nor his pirate Ship, nor his giant Whale, nor the magical Doves of Christmas, he would carry the gifts to all children of the world on... the Christmas Eve Star!"

"Christmas Eve Star!" Mary repeated.

"But is not that the star the Three Kings follow to get to the portal of Bethlehem? If Santa uses it, the Three Kings will be lost!"

"That is true, Lucy! So..."

"If Santa didn't have his sleigh, nor his magical Bicycle, nor his noisy Car, nor his Christmas Train, nor his multi-coloured Balloon, nor his super-fast Plane, nor his pirate Ship, nor his giant Whale, nor the magical Doves of Christmas, nor the Christmas Eve Star... **Dads and Moms** would help Santa bring gifts to all the boys and girls of the world."

"Ohhhhh!" Lucy and Mary exclaimed, astonished.

"Mom... Are you sure that all the Dads and Moms of the world would help Santa Claus if he needed it?" Lucy asked.

"I promise you" her mother replied.

"Then he is sure to bring us gifts! Cool!"

Lucy was very happy, at last compliant.

Lucy and Mary went to bed.

That night they dreamed of the story their mother had told them.

And the next morning...

Merry Christmas!

LUCY'S WORLD
BOOK SERIES

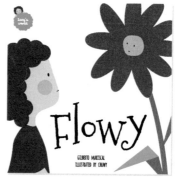

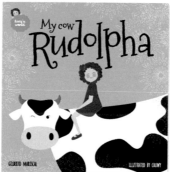

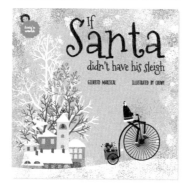

Made in the USA
Lexington, KY
11 December 2018